THIS LITTLE TIGER BOOK BELONGS TO:

_____

_____

_____

_____

The Very Noisy Night

Diana Hendry   Jane Chapman

LITTLE TIGER PRESS
London

It was the middle of the
night, and Big Mouse was
fast asleep in his big bed.
Little Mouse was wide
awake in his little bed.
"Big Mouse! Big Mouse!"
called Little Mouse.
"I can hear something
rushing round the house,
huffing and puffing."

Big Mouse opened one eye and one ear.
"It's only the wind," he said.

"Can I come into your bed?" asked Little Mouse.
"No," said Big Mouse. "There isn't room."
And he turned over and went back to sleep.

Little Mouse lay listening
to the wind. Then, suddenly,
between a huff and a puff,
came a . . .

TAP TAP TAP

TAP

Little Mouse climbed out of bed, opened the
front door — just a crack — and peeped out.

WHOOOSH!

went the wind, but there
was no one outside.
"Big Mouse! Big Mouse!"
called Little Mouse.
"I can hear someone
tapping. Perhaps
there's a burglar
on the roof."

Big Mouse got out of
bed and opened the bedroom
curtains. "Look," he said, "it's
only a branch tapping on the
window. Go back to sleep."
"Can I come into your bed?"
asked Little Mouse.
"No," said Big Mouse.
"You wriggle."

Little Mouse lay in his
own bed and listened
to the wind huffing
and puffing and the
branch tap-tapping —
and someone calling,

"HOO-HOO!
HOO-HOO!"

Little Mouse climbed out of bed again. This time he looked under it. Then he looked in the wardrobe, and feeling very frightened he cried, "Big Mouse! Big Mouse! I think there's a ghost in the house, and it's looking for me. It keeps calling, who who? who who?"

Big Mouse sighed, sat up
and listened. "It's only an owl,"
he said. "It's awake, like you."
"Can I come into your bed?"
asked Little Mouse.
"No," said Big Mouse. "Your
paws are always cold."
And Big Mouse pulled the
blanket over his head and
went back to sleep.

Little Mouse got back into
his own bed and he lay and
listened to the wind
huffing and puffing, the
branch tap-tapping,
and the owl hooting.
But sssh! What
was that?

DRIP DRIP DRIP DRIP

"Big Mouse! Big Mouse!" he called. "I can hear a drip. It's drip-dripping. I think it's raining inside." And Little Mouse jumped out of bed and fetched his red umbrella.

Big Mouse got out of bed too. He opened the
front door. "Be quiet, wind," he said. "Be quiet,
branch. Be quiet, owl." But they took no notice.
Then Big Mouse went into the kitchen, turned
off the dripping tap and put away the umbrella.

"Can I come into your bed?"
asked Little Mouse.
"No, you're nice and snug in your own bed,"
said Big Mouse, taking him back to the bedroom.

Little Mouse lay and listened
to the wind huffing and
puffing, the branch tap-tapping,
and the owl hooting.
And just as he was beginning
to feel very sleepy indeed,
he heard . . .

"WHEEE, WHEEE, WHEEEEE!"

"Big Mouse! Big Mouse!"
he called. "You're snoring."

Wearily Big Mouse got up. He put his ear-muffs on Little Mouse's ears. He put a paper-clip on his own nose, and he went back to bed.

Little Mouse lay and listened to — N o t h i n g !
It was very, very, very quiet. He couldn't hear
the wind huffing or the branch tapping or the owl
hooting or Big Mouse snoring. It was so quiet that
Little Mouse felt he was all alone in the world.

He took off the ear-muffs.
He got out of bed and pulled the paper-clip
off Big Mouse's nose. "Big Mouse! Big Mouse!"
he cried, "I'm lonely!"

Big Mouse flung back
his blanket. "Better come
into my bed," he said.
So Little Mouse hopped
in and his paws were
cold . . .

and he needed just
a little wriggle before
he fell fast asleep.

Big Mouse lay and listened to the wind huffing and puffing and the branch tapping and the owl hooting and Little Mouse snuffling, and very soon he heard the birds waking up. But neither of them heard the alarm clock . . .

BECAUSE THEY WERE
BOTH FAST ASLEEP!

For Emelia, with love
— D.H.

For Anthony, Jane, Mark,
Katy and Alice, with love
— J.C.

LITTLE TIGER PRESS
An imprint of Magi Publications, 1 The Coda Centre,
189 Munster Road, London SW6 6AW
This paperback edition published 1999 · First published in Great Britain 1999
Text © 1999 Diana Hendry · Illustrations © 1999 Jane Chapman
Diana Hendry and Jane Chapman have asserted their rights to be identified
as the author and illustrator of this work under the Copyright,
Designs and Patents Act, 1988
Printed in Singapore · All rights reserved · ISBN 1 85430 609 X
7 9 10 8 6

Join the LITTLE TIGER CLUB now for lots more books to enjoy!

Schools can join too and will receive a special enrolment pack.

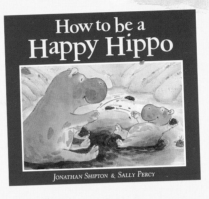

Laura's Star
Klaus Baumgart

Little Tiger's big surprise!
Julie Sykes · Tim Warnes

How to be a Happy Hippo
JONATHAN SHIPTON & SALLY PERCY

The Very Lazy Ladybird
Isobel Finn & Jack Tickle

Join the LITTLE TIGER CLUB now and receive a special Little Tiger goody bag containing badges, pencils and more! Once you become a member you will receive details of special offers, competitions and news of new books. Why not write a book review? The best reviews received will be published on book covers or in the Little Tiger Press catalogue.

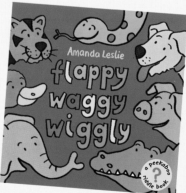

Amanda Leslie
flappy waggy wiggly

a peekaboo riddle book

BABY SEAL ALL ALONE
Linda Cornwell
Gavin Rowe

9948 SQ

LITTLE TIGER CLUB is free to join. Members can cancel their membership at any time, and are under no obligation to purchase any books.
If you would like details of the Little Tiger Club or a catalogue of books please contact:
Little Tiger Press, 1 The Coda Centre, 189 Munster Road, London SW6 6AW, UK. Telephone 020 7385 6333
Visit our website at: www.littletiger.okukbooks.com